COCO

Julie White and Susie Preston

illustrations
Amber Whitney

The Third Alphabet Aliens Adventure

**Let's go on an
Alphabet Aliens Adventure.**

Alphabet Aliens love the alphabet.
And they each have a favorite letter.

Coco's favorite letter is C, of course.

Coco can do lots of cool things that begin with
the letter C. She can cartwheel to the corner,
make candy corn cupcakes and
even dance the can-can.

But do you know the coolest thing Coco can do?

Coco can change color!

All she has to do is close her eyes and count to 10 and she can be any color she likes. She can be the color of a clear blue sky, a cucumber or a candy cane.

She can even change the color of her clothes ... just by counting.

How cool is that?

Changing color makes Coco very good at hide and seek. She can be the color of the curtains, the couch or the carpet.

That's called camouflage and when Coco is camouflaged, she's very hard to find.

Can you find Coco?

Coco has a pet who can change color too. He's a chameleon and his name is Clyde. Clyde can camouflage, just like Coco.

Coco is crazy about Clyde and takes good care of her chameleon. She keeps his cage clean and cozy with lots of cushions. And she cooks him delicious casseroles, cakes and cookies.

Clyde is crazy about cookies, and Coco is clever at creating crazy cookie combinations.

One day she came up with the idea of a cotton candy cookie covered in crunchy cabbage.

Critters love cabbage in their cookies!

Before long, the cookies were cooling on the counter.

Clyde counted exactly 12 cookies. Clyde was learning to count and he especially liked counting cookies.

"Let's play catch while the cookies cool," said Coco.

And off they went.

When they came back to check the cookies, Clyde counted again. This time he counted 9 cookies.

"How can that be?" thought Clyde. "Didn't I count correctly?"

"It's okay, Clyde," said Coco. "You were close enough. Now let's have a cookie."

And they did.

Coco's next cookie combination was cabbage and carrot coated in caramel.

This time, Coco helped Clyde with the counting. There were exactly 20 cookies.

"Let's cartwheel to the corner while the cookies cool," said Coco.

And off they went.

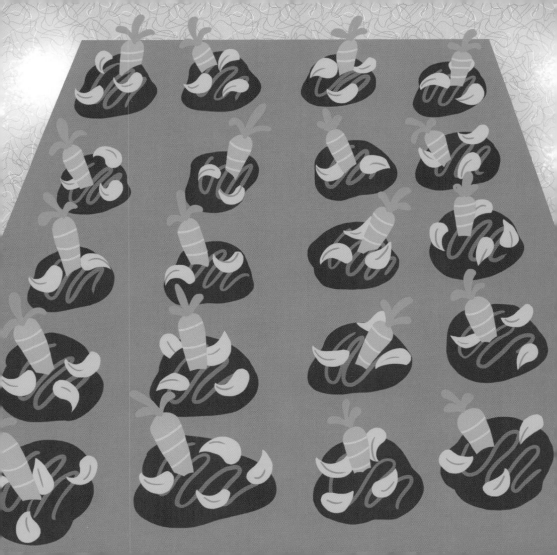

When they came back to the kitchen, it was clear that some cookies were missing.

Coco and Clyde counted. Only 15 cookies. "I know we counted correctly the first time," said Coco. "There were 20 cookies."

Coco was confused. Then Coco looked more closely.

And there they were ....

Clues!

Claw prints criss-crossing all over the counter and a trail of cookie crumbs leading to the window.

"Crikey!" cried Coco. "Some critter is swiping our cookies."

"Come on, Clyde. Let's catch this critter in the act!"

So Coco baked another batch of cabbage and carrot cookies and left them on the counter.

But this time, Coco and Clyde didn't cartwheel or play catch while the cookies were cooling.

This time Coco and Clyde camouflaged.

Coco closed her eyes, counted to 10 and turned crimson – the exact color of the curtains.

And so did Clyde.

Then Coco and Clyde stood close to the curtains, completely camouflaged, and waited for the critter to come.

Pretty soon they heard the sound of claws clicking on concrete. Then they caught sight of a critter creeping through the kitchen window, past the curtains.

It was the calico cat from the corner. And he couldn't believe his luck. Another batch of cabbage and carrot cookies!

The cat couldn't see Coco and Clyde, but Coco and Clyde could see him.

They waited as he crept along the counter, closer and closer to the cookies, until Coco suddenly cried, "CAUGHT YA!"

"YEEEEEOW!" That was one confounded cat!

He catapulted out the window as fast as he could!

"Congratulations, Clyde!" cried Coco. "I don't think any more critters will be coming for our cookies."

"Let's play croquet while the cookies finish cooling."

And off they went.

Mmmmm ... cookies!